MARIANNA MAYER

Young Jesus of Nazareth

MORROW JUNIOR BOOKS · NEW YORK

ACKNOWLEDGMENTS

The author would like to extend thanks to the following:
the Reverend Jennings Matheson and Elvira Charles, for their thoughtful readings
of the manuscript; Janice Ostan at SuperStock, for all her efforts researching so many
important images for this book; Christopher Spooner, for his help in the preliminary
stages of the project; and Dan Siemiakoski, assistant manager of Cowley and
Cathedral Books in Boston, who pointed out certain materials of interest.

✦   ✦   ✦   ✦   ✦   ✦   ✦

The text type is 17-point Jensen.

Copyright © 1999 by Marianna Mayer

Published by Morrow Junior Books
a division of William Morrow and Company, Inc.
1350 Avenue of the Americas, New York, NY 10019
www.williammorrow.com

Printed in Hong Kong by South China Printing Company (1988) Ltd.

10 9 8 7 6 5 4 3 2 1

Library of Congress Cataloging-in-Publication Data
Mayer, Marianna.
Young Jesus of Nazareth / Marianna Mayer.
p. cm.
Includes bibliographical references.
Summary: Presents a picture of the early life of Jesus
and the signs that revealed him as a very extraordinary child.
ISBN 0-688-16727-6 (trade)—ISBN 0-688-16728-4 (library)
1. Jesus Christ—Childhood—Juvenile literature.
[1. Jesus Christ—Childhood.] I. Title.
BT320.M35 1999 232.92'7—dc21 98-47474 CIP AC

IT WAS A HUMBLE BEGINNING. In a stable surrounded by farm animals, Mary the Virgin gave birth to the infant Jesus.

N THE BLESSED NIGHT that Christ was born, a radiant star shone down on the little town of Bethlehem, where the holy child lay in a manger. Angels on high sang of his miraculous birth, and the shepherds in the field heard the chorus. When they gazed up at the star, a cloud of light descended from the heavens. As the wondrous cloud drew near, it took on the shape of celestial figures, and the singing grew clearer.

Then an angel stood before the shepherds and said, "Fear not. I bring tidings of great joy to all people. Today is born a Savior, who is Christ the Lord. This shall be a sign to you. You shall find the infant laid in a manger."

Led by the star, the shepherds came upon a stable. There they found Mary and Joseph, and in the manger was the holy child. The shepherds brought gifts for the Savior—baskets of fresh eggs, ripe figs, apricots, and earthen jars of sage-scented honey.

IN MANY PLACES of the land strange happenings gave signs of the holy event. That evening in Rome a geyser burst forth from the earth. A temple roof collapsed without warning, shattering a magnificent statue of the Roman deity Jupiter. And a statue of Venus declared to the frightened people in the temple: "This has happened because a virgin conceived a son and has given birth this day."

The Roman Emperor Augustus was standing on a hill nearby when suddenly he saw a vision in the sky of a virgin encircled by a rainbow, with her child soaring above. Augustus sought out his oracles for an explanation. "A holy child has been born," he was told, "before whom all must give praise." Then the emperor ordered an altar to be placed on the hill, and dedicated it to the Firstborn of God.

All through that night and into the dawn the hearts of good people filled with joy. Animals of every kind grew peaceful; flowers, herbs, and shrubs burst with new growth; and trees bloomed, scattering their sweet fragrance across the land.

Far to the east three wise kings saw the star of Bethlehem rising. They knew from their study of the constellations that this was a sign of the coming of a great king. They set out at once to follow where the star might lead.

"Where is the infant king of the Jews?" the wise men asked those in the city of Jerusalem. "We saw his star as it rose and have come to see him."

When King Herod received word of their inquiries, he grew anxious, for he worried that this newborn king would seize his throne. Herod quickly summoned the three wise men. Concealing his fears with false smiles, he asked to know the exact date that the star had appeared and then bade them a safe journey, saying, "Go learn all you can. And when you have found the child, let me know, so that I may pay him my respects."

The three kings followed the star until at last it halted over the stable where the child lay. They humbly knelt before the babe and brought forth their treasures: gifts of gold, frankincense, and myrrh.

That night an angel warned the three kings not to go back to Herod, and so they returned to their own country by a different route.

Soon Mary and Joseph traveled to Jerusalem to present the infant Jesus to the priests at the temple for the customary blessing. But the priests objected when they heard the name chosen for the child, since Jesus means "God is with us."

Joseph told them firmly, "A messenger of the Lord came to me and said, 'Name the child Jesus, for he is the one who is to save his people.'"

The priests prayed for guidance. Then Simeon, the eldest priest, saw an angel holding a stone tablet with Jesus' name written upon it, and he declared to the others: "Indeed, the child's chosen name is pleasing to the Lord."

After the sacred ceremony was performed, Joseph and Mary planned to take the newborn baby Jesus back home to Nazareth. But that night an angel awakened Joseph. "Take the child and his mother, and escape into Egypt," said the angel. "For Herod intends to search for the child and do away with him."

Joseph sprang from bed. Quickly he woke Mary, and with the baby they fled under cover of darkness for the distant land of Egypt.

Herod was enraged when the three wise men failed to return. The king ordered his soldiers to go into Bethlehem and all the surrounding districts, and kill every male child who was under two years of age.

Jesus' cousin John, who had recently been born to the elderly Elizabeth, would have perished if the Lord had not sent one of his angels to her. Heeding the angel's warning, Elizabeth escaped with her son and hid in a cave until she could safely follow the Holy Family into Egypt.

WITH ONLY ONE DONKEY

and few provisions, the Holy Family faced a long and dangerous journey. It was not long before they lost their way in the vast desert between Palestine and Egypt. Late in the day fierce lions approached them. Unafraid, the infant stretched out his tiny hand to the wild creatures. The lions were tamed by the child's gentle touch and guided the Holy Family back on the path to Egypt.

But their hardships grew truly grave when their small supply of fruit, bread, and water was exhausted. Then one evening the Holy Family stumbled upon the camp of a group of robbers. The leader was a ruthless man, but when he gazed into the infant's eyes, his hard heart softened toward the desperate travelers. He took the Holy Family into his hut, and his wife gave them food. Mary soon prepared to bathe her infant in a basin of fresh water.

Seeing this, the leader said to his wife, "Mark me, this is no ordinary child. Ask his mother if we may wash our sick child in the water she has used. I believe it will heal our boy." The child had been stricken with leprosy since birth, and as soon as he was placed in the same water, his painful sores disappeared and he was healed.

The next morning the travelers were given fresh supplies and led back on the path to Egypt.

As the Holy Family approached the delta of the Nile, they came upon a tall, spreading date tree. While they camped there for the night, the tree bent its branches low so that the child could easily pick its fruit.

The following morning a flock of tiny fluttering birds gathered around the mother and child and perched on their shoulders and hands. Their playful antics and songs filled Mary with happiness and made her son laugh with delight.

Finally the arduous journey was at an end, and the weary family arrived in the fertile land of Egypt.

T FIRST LIFE IN EGYPT was not easy for them. Joseph had to set up a workshop and struggled to find work as a carpenter. To help support them, Mary returned to the beautiful needlework she had done as a girl while living in the temple in Nazareth. Word of her craft spread, and soon she had many requests for her exquisitely embroidered altar cloths and tapestries. With the baby Jesus by her side, she spent long hours each day sewing.

When she was not busy with chores, Mary told her son stories to entertain him. She and Joseph marveled at how quickly he began to speak and the swiftness with which he learned.

Still, it took time for the child and those around him to come to understand his extraordinary divine power. One morning when Jesus was five years old, a priest observed him making sparrows out of clay on the Sabbath. When he pointed out that the child was working on a day no labor was to be performed, Jesus clapped his hands. At once the clay figures sprang to life and flew away.

At this time Joseph felt that Jesus was so bright that he should be sent to a teacher. But all attempts to educate the child proved baffling to his instructors. They tried to teach him the Greek alphabet, but Jesus became impatient and refused. Finally he said, "I already know the letters you're trying to teach me. To you they are like empty bronze pitchers or a clashing of cymbals, which can't produce glory or wisdom because it is all noise." And then he very quickly recited the letters from alpha to omega.

When the teachers heard the child speak, they sent the boy back to Joseph, saying, "This child is barely five years old, and yet he says things that even we do not understand. The truth is, we have never met anyone like him."

AT THE AGE OF SIX, Jesus was playing on the rooftop of a house with some children when a boy named Zenon slipped and fell to his death. Frightened, the other children ran away, leaving Jesus there alone.

When the grief-stricken parents of the dead child accused Jesus of causing the accident, he said, "I didn't throw him down." Then Jesus jumped from the roof and stood by the body of the boy. He called to him in a loud voice, "Zenon! Get up and trouble your parents no further."

At once the child got up and ran to embrace his mother and father. And the crowd that had witnessed this marvel declared to Mary and Joseph that Jesus was a worker of miracles.

Not long after, Mary sent Jesus to draw water from the well. But as he was carrying the pitcher filled with water, he lost his grip and it fell, breaking into many pieces. With barely a pause, Jesus spread out his thin cloak and, filling it with water, carried it to his mother without losing a single drop. Seeing this miracle, Mary kissed and thanked him; but she kept to herself all such mysteries she had seen.

When Elizabeth arrived in Egypt with her young son, John, Mary was overjoyed to welcome her mother's sister. Now Jesus had a constant playmate close to his own age, and the boys spent hours together exploring the countryside. Their companions were the wild creatures of the desert. Soon they befriended some small swift deer with long graceful necks and clear dark eyes. The gentle animals followed the children wherever they went and ate from their hands without fear. Birds of every kind loved to alight upon the boys' shoulders and playfully tug at their hair as the children fed and talked to them.

While in the desert, young John and Jesus met a holy man who lived a hard and solitary life as a hermit. They often returned to visit him and sat engrossed as he told them ancient tales and parables.

SOON AFTER JESUS turned eight years old, an angel came to Joseph and said, "Herod the tyrant is dead. Now it is safe to take the child and his mother into the land of Israel once more."

Joyfully, Joseph and Mary prepared to leave Egypt without delay. Together they distributed their household goods and furnishings among the poor. The few things they would need Joseph packed on the faithful donkey that had traveled with them from Palestine.

The news of their departure spread quickly, and the friends they had made while in Egypt gathered around to say their good-byes. Missing but in their thoughts was Elizabeth, who had passed away a few years earlier. On the day the Holy Family arranged to leave, young John told them he wished to remain behind in the desert with the old hermit. Mary and Joseph were sorry not to take John with them, but they accepted his decision, understanding that it was time for him to follow his own destiny. Jesus embraced his cousin, and John promised that they would one day meet again.

Established once more in their homeland, Joseph prospered as a carpenter. Jesus was now old enough to help and soon learned the trade.

In the spring, the child and his father planted grain in the family's small field. While Joseph sowed most of the grain, Jesus managed only one small portion. But when Jesus' crop was harvested and threshed, Joseph shook his head in wonder, for it yielded one hundred times its measure. Then, beckoning the poor in the village, Jesus made them a gift of the bounty.

The following year, Joseph received an important order from a wealthy man to make a bed. Joseph went into the forest and cut the wood himself, but when he returned to his workshop he realized that he had mistakenly cut one board shorter than the rest. Then Jesus, seeing his father's distress, said, "Put the boards down and line them up at one end."

Joseph did, and then he watched as Jesus took hold of the shorter board, and, by stretching it, made it the same length as the rest.

Soon after this incident, an infant girl in the village became sick and died, and the mother grieved terribly. Jesus heard the woman weeping while he was out playing, and he went to her.

When he discovered that the baby was dead, he touched the child's chest and said, "I say to you, little one, don't die but live, and be with your mother."

Immediately the infant opened her eyes and began to laugh. Those looking on declared, "This boy is a god or some heavenly messenger sent by the Lord."

But Jesus walked away and resumed playing, taking no notice of their praise.

THE YEAR OF JESUS' TWELFTH BIRTHDAY, his family and their relatives went to Jerusalem for the Passover festival. On their journey home, Jesus slipped away from the traveling party. His parents began asking for him among their relatives. Unable to find him, they grew very frightened indeed and returned at once to the city in search of him.

After three long days, the distraught parents discovered Jesus in the temple, sitting among the teachers, listening to the law and questioning them. All eyes were on the twelve-year-old. Every scholar was astounded that he, a mere boy, could interrogate them and explain the holy law and the parables of the prophets like a great wise man.

Ignoring the crowd that had gathered around her son, Mary rushed to Jesus and cried, "Why have you worried us so? Don't you know we have been frantic to find you?"

But Jesus only gazed at her in surprise. "Why were you searching for me?" he asked at last. "Don't you know that I have to be in my father's house?"

The scholars then approached Mary. "You are to be praised," they said, "for God has blessed you in giving you this boy as your son. In all our days we have never seen or heard such glorious virtue and wisdom."

Then Jesus obediently got up and left for home with his mother and Joseph.

WHEN JESUS WAS a few years older, there was news of his cousin John's arrival at the Jordan River. Reports said that after living in the wilderness as a hermit, he had become a great prophet who wore rough rags and ate only raw honey, and that by the river Jordan he was baptizing people to wash away their sins. All of Jerusalem, including the priests and holy men, went out to him to be baptized, and those who did said that it changed their hearts forever.

Then Jesus went to John at the banks of the river to be baptized. John tried to stop him, saying, "I am the one who should be baptized by you, yet you come to me."

But Jesus said to him, "This is as it should be for now."

John bowed to Jesus' wish. After he baptized Jesus with the waters from the river, the heavens suddenly opened up. Then those standing there saw the Lord's spirit come down to Jesus like a dove. As it alighted on him, there was a voice from the skies that said, "This is my favored son—in whom I am well pleased!"

THEN JESUS WENT on to travel all over Galilee, teaching in the temples and proclaiming the news of heaven's imperial rule. His reputation quickly swept throughout the land. Everyone who was ill or suffering went to him, and all these he cured. Huge crowds flocked to follow him from Galilee, Jerusalem, Judea, and from across the Jordan.

With the crowds behind him, Jesus climbed up a lofty mountain. When he reached the top, he sat down and his disciples gathered around him. Jesus then began to speak, and this is what he wanted to teach them:

BLESSED ARE THE POOR,
FOR HEAVEN BELONGS TO THEM.

✦

BLESSED ARE THOSE WHO GRIEVE,
FOR THEY WILL BE CONSOLED.

✦

BLESSED ARE THE GENTLE,
FOR THEY SHALL INHERIT THE EARTH.

✦

BLESSED ARE THOSE WHO HUNGER FOR JUSTICE,
FOR THEY SHALL BE FED.

✦

BLESSED ARE THE MERCIFUL,
FOR THEY WILL RECEIVE MERCY.

✦

BLESSED ARE THE PURE OF HEART,
FOR THEY SHALL SEE GOD.

✦

BLESSED ARE THOSE WHO WORK FOR PEACE, FOR
THEY SHALL BE KNOWN AS GOD'S CHILDREN.

✦

BLESSED ARE THOSE WHO HAVE SUFFERED PERSECUTION
FOR THE SAKE OF JUSTICE, FOR HEAVEN'S DOMAIN BELONGS TO THEM.

AUTHOR'S NOTE

Although we do not have any historically reliable stories about Jesus before he was about age thirty, a few conclusions may be derived from the New Testament gospels. He was probably born very near the end of the reign of Herod the Great, shortly before 4 B.C. His parents were Jewish, and their names were Mary and Joseph. Jesus grew up in the tiny town of Nazareth, in the hills of southern Galilee, about a hundred miles north of Jerusalem. Nazareth was less than four miles from the cosmopolitan city of Sepphoris, which had a population of forty thousand. Trade with other parts of the Mediterranean was extensive, and it is probable that most Jews were bilingual, speaking both Aramaic and Greek. Since 63 B.C., the whole of Palestine had been part of the Roman Empire.

Within the New Testament, the birth of Jesus is referred to only in two places—the gospels of Matthew and Luke, both written within the last twenty years of the first century. However, these two gospels differ significantly. In Matthew, the family lives in Bethlehem and moves to Nazareth after returning from the flight to Egypt. In Luke, the family lives in Nazareth and travels to Bethlehem because of the census, and Jesus is born in a stable en route, after which the family returns to Nazareth. In Matthew, the guiding star appears to the wise men, and in Luke's version, the angels sing of Jesus' birth to the shepherds. In Matthew, King Herod orders the slaughter of male infants in Bethlehem, forcing the family to seek refuge in Egypt. In Luke, there is no such slaughter or flight.

Most scholars conclude that the differences between the two gospels illustrate that the birth stories are symbolic narratives whose details reflect the themes most important to Matthew and Luke. For example, Matthew emphasizes Jesus' kingship by tracing Jesus' genealogy through the kings of Israel, concluding with a story of three kings who seek one who is born greater than themselves—the "king of the Jews." Luke, on the other hand, traces Jesus' genealogy back through the prophets, and uses the shepherds—the common people—as the group to whom the news of the birth comes, emphasizing Jesus' role as a radical social prophet.

Though these birth stories demonstrate that Jesus was an extraordinary being, they do not tell us what sort of child he might have been. To construct a portrait of that child, I turned to the Infancy Gospel of Thomas. Legends of Jesus' youth developed in the early centuries of Christianity and were continually expanded from late antiquity to the Middle Ages; this particular late first- or second-century gospel consists of a series of episodes in which Jesus is portrayed as a quite human, very childlike boy. At first he is revealed to be a strong-minded youth and a prodigy, an enigma to his limited and merely mortal teachers. As he grows, he becomes eager to use his divine power to help and heal those in need.

Along with the stories found in the canonical Bible and in the apocrypha (early Christian writings not included in the New Testament), to a lesser extent material was also derived from the revelations of the Venerated Anne Catherine Emmerich. Though not recognized as part of the Bible or Christian doctrine, her visionary writings were considered to be in harmony with tradition and the Holy Scripture. Such writings were sometimes published with an imprimatur (an authorization by the Roman Catholic Church indicating material with no contradiction to doctrine). It is believed by some theologians that God allowed such revelations as a powerful means of spreading and strengthening Christian faith.

SOURCE NOTES

The tales of the strange portents in Rome at the time of Christ's birth and the story about Emperor Augustus first appeared in A.D. 418 in *The Universal History of Orosius*, a document written by a friend of St. Augustine. From the Venerated Anne Catherine Emmerich's visions comes the story of John and Elizabeth's escape into Egypt as well as Mary's occupation with her child and her needlework while in Egypt. All of the childhood miracles of Jesus in Egypt and in Nazareth are from the Infancy Gospel of Thomas. The descriptions of John and Jesus' childhood friendship are from *The New Testament Apocrypha* (The Child Jesus and John, New Testament Apocrypha; The Life of John According to Serapion; and The Gospel of Pseudo-Matthew); and the Holy Family's encounters in the desert are from *The New Testament Apocrypha* (The Gospel of Pseudo-Matthew and the Arabic Gospel of the Infancy). All other stories are derived from the gospels of Matthew and Luke.

SELECTED BIBLIOGRAPHY

Aron, Robert. *A Boy Named Jesus.* Berkeley, Calif.: Ulysses Press, 1997.

Borg, Maruc J. *Meeting Jesus Again for the First Time: The Historical Jesus and the Heart of Contemporary Faith.* New York: HarperCollins, 1994.

*Emmerich, Anne Catherine. *The Life of Christ and the Biblical Revelations,* in four volumes. Rockford, Ill.: Tan Books, 1986.

Hock, Ronald F. *The Infancy Gospels of James and Thomas.* Santa Rosa, Calif.: Polebridge Press, 1995.

*Mary of Agreda. *The Mystical City of God,* in four volumes. Rockford, Ill.: Tan Books, 1972.

Miller, Robert J., ed. *The Complete Gospels* (Annotated Scholars Version). Santa Rosa, Calif.: Polebridge Press, 1994.

Patterson, Stephen J. *The Gospels of Thomas and Jesus.* Santa Rosa, Calif.: Polebridge Press, 1993.

Schneemelcher, Wilhelm, ed. *Gospels and Related Writings,* revised edition. Vol. 1 of *New Testament Apocrypha.* Louisville, Ky.: Westminster/John Knox Press, 1990.

Wood, Christopher. *Tissot.* London, England: Weidenfeld & Nicolson, 1986.

*Titles denoted with * indicate sources with an imprimatur.*

LIST OF ILLUSTRATIONS

Many of the paintings in this book are the work of James Tissot (1836–1902). A successful artist in both France and England often commissioned to create portraits of the wealthy, Tissot stopped into a church one day to "catch the atmosphere for a picture" and experienced a religious conversion. Thereafter, he devoted much of his efforts to religious subjects. Using the Bible and the visionary writings of the Venerated Anne Catherine Emmerich as inspiration, he traveled to the Holy Land in search of exact historical locations and period detail. In eight years he produced 365 illustrations depicting sites of biblical events, clothing, and hairstyles as authentically as possible. Much of the other artwork that appears in this book depicts the biblical characters in settings and costumes of the artists' own place and day, in order to bring the religious stories closer to their own lives.

Front jacket: Heinrich Hoffman. *Christ in the Temple at Twelve.* Private collection (SuperStock). ◆ back jacket: Carlo Dolci. *The Christ Child.* Private collection (SuperStock). ◆ page 1: Fra Angelico. *The Christ Child from the Madonna of the San Pietro.* Florence, Italy: Museo di San Marco (Bridgeman Art Library International). ◆ page 3: James Tissot. *The Birth of Jesus Christ.* Brooklyn, NY: Brooklyn Museum (SuperStock). ◆ page 4: James Tissot. *The Angels and the Shepherds.* Brooklyn, NY: Brooklyn Museum (SuperStock). ◆ page 5: Gerrit van Honthorst. *Adoration of the Child.* Florence, Italy: Uffizi (Scala/Art Resource). ◆ page 6: Antoine Caron. *Augustus and the Tiburtine Sibyl.* Paris, France: Musée du Louvre (SuperStock). ◆ page 7: James Tissot. *The Wise and Herod.* Brooklyn, NY: Brooklyn Museum (SuperStock). ◆ page 8: Edward Burne-Jones and William Morris & Co. *The Adoration of the Magi.* St. Petersburg, Russia: Hermitage (Bridgeman Art Library International). ◆ page 9: Fra Bartolomeo. *Presentation of Christ in the Temple.* Vienna, Austria: Kunsthistorisches Museum (Erich Lessing/Art Resource). ◆ page 10: James Tissot. *Vision of Joseph.* Brooklyn, NY: Brooklyn Museum (SuperStock). ◆ page 11: James Tissot. *The Flight into Egypt.* Brooklyn, NY: Brooklyn Museum (SuperStock). ◆ page 12: Albrecht Durer. *The Lion.* Private collection (A.K.G. Berlin/SuperStock). ◆ page 13: Jacopo Bassano. *The Flight into Egypt.* Christie's Images (Bridgeman Art Library International). ◆ page 14: Juan de Borgona. *The Flight into Egypt.* Cuenca, Spain: Museo Catedralicio (Bridgeman Art Library International). ◆ page 15: Caravaggio. *Rest on the Flight into Egypt.* Rome, Italy: Galleria Doria Pamphili (Scala/Art Resource). ◆ page 16: James Tissot. *Sojourn in Egypt.* Brooklyn, NY: Brooklyn Museum (SuperStock). ◆ page 17: Artist unknown. *The Holy Family in Joseph's Carpentry Shop* (from Book of Hours, Spain, late fifteenth century). London, England: British Library (Art Resource). ◆ page 18: Francisco de Zurbaran. *The Holy Family.* Madrid, Spain: Private collection (Peter Willi/ Bridgeman Art Library International). ◆ page 19: Francisco de Zurbaran. *The Christ Child.* Moscow, Russia: Pushkin Museum of Fine Arts (SuperStock). ◆ page 20: Bartolomeo Esteban Murillo. *The Children with the Shell (Christ Child and Saint John the Baptist).* Madrid, Spain: Museo del Prado (Scala/Art Resource). ◆ page 21: James Tissot. *Childhood of John the Baptist.* Brooklyn, NY: Brooklyn Museum (SuperStock). ◆ page 22: James Tissot. *The Return from Egypt.* Brooklyn, NY: Brooklyn Museum (SuperStock). ◆ page 24: John Rogers Herbert. *The Youth of Our Lord.* London, England: Guildhall Art Gallery (SuperStock). ◆ page 25: Sir John Everett Millais. *Christ in the House of His Parents.* London, England: Tate Gallery (Tate Gallery, London/Art Resource). ◆ page 27: James Tissot. *Jesus Sitting in the Midst of the Doctors.* Brooklyn, NY: Brooklyn Museum (SuperStock). ◆ page 28: James Tissot. *Christ's Exhortation to the Twelve Apostles.* Brooklyn, NY: Brooklyn Museum (SuperStock). ◆ page 29: James Tissot. *Baptism of Jesus.* Brooklyn, NY: Brooklyn Museum (SuperStock). ◆ page 31: Leonardo da Vinci. *Head of the Savior.* Madrid, Spain: Museo Lazaro Galdiano (Giraudon/Art Resource).